Stacy Gregg (Ngāti Mahuta/Ngāti Pukeko) is the author of Pony Club Secrets, the inspiration for the major TV series MYSTIC. www.stacygregg.co.uk

Books by Stacy Gregg

The Spellbound Ponies series

MAGIC AND MISCHIEF
SUGAR AND SPICE

The Pony Club Secrets series

MYSTIC AND THE MIDNIGHT RIDE
BLAZE AND THE DARK RIDER
DESTINY AND THE WILD HORSES
STARDUST AND THE DAREDEVIL PONIES
COMET AND THE CHAMPION'S CUP
STORM AND THE SILVER BRIDLE
FORTUNE AND THE GOLDEN TROPHY
VICTORY AND THE ALL-STARS ACADEMY
FLAME AND THE REBEL RIDERS
ANGEL AND THE FLYING STALLIONS
LIBERTY AND THE DREAM RIDE
NIGHTSTORM AND THE GRAND SLAM
ISSIE AND THE CHRISTMAS PONY

Pony Club Rival series

THE AUDITIONS
SHOWJUMPERS
RIDING STAR
THE PRIZE

For older readers

THE PRINCESS AND THE FOAL
THE ISLAND OF LOST HORSES
THE GIRL WHO RODE THE WIND
THE DIAMOND HORSE
THE THUNDERBOLT PONY
THE FIRE STALLION
PRINCE OF PONIES
THE FOREVER HORSE

Spellbound Ponies

Sugar and Spice

STACY GREGG

HarperCollins *Children's Books*

First published in Great Britain by
HarperCollins *Children's Books* in 2021
HarperCollins *Children's Books* is a division of HarperCollins*Publishers* Ltd
HarperCollins Publishers
1 London Bridge Street
London SE1 9GF

www.harpercollins.co.uk

HarperCollins*Publishers*
1st Floor, Watermarque Building, Ringsend Road
Dublin 4, Ireland

1

ISBN 978-0-00-840290-7

Stacy Gregg and Crush Creative assert the moral right to be identified as the
author and illustrator of the work respectively.

A CIP catalogue record for this title is available from the British Library.

Typeset in Cambria Regular 12/24
Printed and bound in England by CPI Group (UK) Ltd, Croydon CR0 4YY

MIX
Paper from
responsible sources
FSC™ C007454

For India, who makes a mean-as pav

Chapter One

It was such a lovely day for a picnic! Olivia had a spring in her step as she walked from her house to Pemberley Stables with her lunchbox packed to the brim with ham sandwiches and chocolate cake.

The stables, ancient and ivy-clad, looked for all the world as if nobody had set foot inside them for centuries. But Olivia had been here before and she knew that the heavy wooden doors would slide open easily for her. She stepped inside and admired her handiwork. She'd been on a cleaning spree lately. The musty cobwebs were gone and the cobblestones in the corridor had been polished until they gleamed.

'Eliza? It's me!' Olivia whispered into the gloom. 'I've brought us picnic treats. Sandwiches and cake!'

'Cake? Oh, how glorious!' The voice came from right behind her and Olivia spun round. Standing there, where a moment ago there had been nothing but thin air, was a girl dressed in an old-fashioned white Georgian nightgown with a tangled mass of red curls tied up in a bun and bright green eyes. She looked about the same age

♥ 10 ♥

as Olivia, which was nine, but, in fact, she was two hundred and nine on account of the fact that she was a ghost!

'Oh, not those old clothes again, Eliza!' Olivia squeaked. 'I've bought you a new set to wear,' she said, handing over a bundle of new things. 'And don't sneak up on me like that!'

'Oops, sorry, Livvy!' The red-haired girl giggled. 'I didn't mean to startle you. And it's frightfully nice of you to bring me clothes, and lunch . . .'

At that moment there was a whinny from inside the first stall and a beautiful jet-black pony stuck her head out over the bottom door. 'Bess, on the other hand,'

Eliza grinned, 'simply cannot wait to munch on some scrummy pony food!'

'Well, she's in luck!' Olivia said. 'The hay is on its way. I ordered a bale from **Harrow's Horse Feed** this morning.'

As she said this, there was a honk outside.

'Hay, hay, hooray!' Olivia said. 'That'll be the delivery now!'

She bounded outside and found Mr Harrow standing in the driveway, a clipboard in his hand, looking quite confused.

'Are you the girl who ordered the hay?' he asked.

'Yes!' Olivia said brightly. 'Can you stack it inside, please? I've cleared a space.'

Mr Harrow still looked puzzled as he grabbed a bale from the truck.

'I didn't think they were any horses in these stables,' he said as he lugged it inside. 'They've been abandoned for as long as anyone can remember.'

'Well, not any more!' Olivia said cheerily. 'We've only got Bess right now, but we're expecting lots more ponies very soon.'

'Is that so?' said Mr Harrow. 'Well, you'll be needing more hay then!'

'More?' Olivia had already emptied the entire contents of her piggy bank to buy this one bale.

'Oh yes,' Mr Harrow said seriously. 'Ponies will eat you out of house and home, you know!'

Mr Harrow threw the bale down and headed back out. He was about to leave when he spotted the words carved into the stone wall half hidden beneath the overgrown ivy. 'Hang on a minute –' he pushed the leaves aside – 'there's something written under here . . .'

Mr Harrow read the words out loud.

The deepest magic binds these stables
Unless two brave girls can turn the tables.
The curse on each horse must be found,
Then break their spell to be unbound.

'What's that all about then? Is it a poem?'

'Erm, yes, something like that,' Olivia replied.

In fact, it wasn't a poem at all. It was a spell. And

Olivia knew the spooky story behind it only too well.

It had all begun two hundred years earlier when Lady Luella, owner of Pemberley Manor, had decided to go fox-hunting. Her daughter, Eliza, had begged to come with her on the hunt. Eliza was an excellent rider and everything was going brilliantly until they struck a rabbit hole at a hedge jump and Eliza's pony, Chessie, lost his footing and fell.

Eliza's death so devastated Lady Luella that she had decided to punish all the ponies in the stables. She had paid the Pemberley Witch to cast a curse over them all and ever since then the stables had been spellbound. The witch's magic kept the poor ponies trapped forever in time!

Except there was a weakness in the witch's spell. *Two brave girls* could break the curse, and Olivia, who was very brave indeed, was one of those girls. The other was Lady Luella's daughter, Eliza. After her terrible accident, Eliza had refused to leave the Spellbound ponies, staying on at the stables as their groom, and that was how she met Olivia.

When Olivia had helped Eliza to free Bad Bess, the naughty highway pony, from the witch's spell, the two girls had become firm friends.

Having a ghost as a friend was a lot of fun, but there were drawbacks. For starters there was Eliza's rather worrying habit of coming and going in a magical *poof*! Right now, as Mr Harrow stood in the doorway of the darkened stables, Olivia became aware that a spooky swirl of mist was starting to rise – a sure sign that Eliza was about to mystically materialise! Yikes! Olivia was pretty sure she was the only one who could actually see this happening, but she wasn't taking any chances!

'It's been lovely chatting with you about poetry and all that,' Olivia said, hurrying Mr Harrow out to his truck and helping him by opening the door, 'but I've got a pony to feed!'

'Of course, of course,' Mr Harrow agreed. 'I'd best be going anyway. Lots more deliveries to make.'

As he drove away, Mr Harrow heard the faint tinkle of ghostly laughter, and a shiver made its way down his spine. Mr Harrow, who was not the sort of man to believe in ghosts, shrugged it off and checked his notebook to see who was next on the list.

Meanwhile, inside the stables, one of those ghosts he didn't believe in was sitting on the hay bale and giggling with delight as Olivia fed a biscuit of it to Bess.

'They suit you,' Olivia said, nodding to Eliza's new clothes.

'Thanks.' Eliza grinned. 'She's really enjoying it, isn't she?' she said, looking at Bess as the mare took a hungry mouthful.

Bess was the only horse the girls had set free so

far. When she had been spellbound Bess had been a highway pony and had led a naughty life of crime. But now the spell was broken Bess was a perfectly normal horse. The only sign of her wayward past was the black mask and velvet cape that still hung in her stall.

'Ponies do eat a lot,' Olivia noted with concern. 'How will I afford to keep her in hay?'

'Oh, you'll find a way!' Eliza said confidently. 'Come on, Livvy! Time for us to free another pony from the witch's spell. Are you ready to cross the threshold once more?'

Each loosebox in the stables belonged to an enchanted pony. All you had to do to summon them was to walk through their stall door and say their name.

'I'm ready,' Olivia said.

They stepped up to the next stall. The brass plaque on the door gave off an unearthly glow and the pony's name materialised in front of their eyes.

'Ooooh,' Eliza said. 'How exciting! The pony you are about to meet was once the fastest racehorse in Spellbound Stables. I wonder what the witch's enchantment has done to him?'

'Let's find out,' Olivia said.

She had goose bumps all over as she stepped through the door and spoke the name out loud.

'Prince!'

Chapter Two

As Olivia said Prince's name, a ghostly fog rose up from the straw and soon filled the entire stall.

'Eliza!' Olivia cried.

'Livvy!' Eliza called back. 'I'm right here!'

Olivia reached out to grasp her hand, but her fingers slipped right through as if her best friend was made of smoke.

'So where is Prince? He must be here somewhere.'

Eliza was utterly excited as she felt her way around in the darkness. 'Oh, just wait until you meet him, Livvy! He's so amazing! Back in the day when Pemberley Stables weren't spellbound, Prince was my very favourite horse in the whole place. He's terribly swift, the fastest horse in all of Pemberley. And so stunning – dappled grey! You've never seen such a sleek, powerful racing machine! Why, I would wager—'

'Ick!' Olivia shrieked. 'Yuck! I just stood in something squishy!'

'What-ho? Oh no!' a voice right beside her wailed. **'You've gone and put your foot in it, haven't you?'**

At that moment the fog cleared and Olivia looked down to see a gooey mess of yellow gunk on her boot.

'What on earth is that?'

'Why, lemon meringue pie, of course!'

Standing right there in front of the girls was the chubbiest pony Olivia had ever seen.

'**Eliza!**' the pony cried out with delight. '**Well, I never! My dearest old chum! How lovely to see you here! Only I wish you hadn't brought old Clod-foot with you! Look what she did to my pie!**'

'Hey!' Olivia said. 'That's a bit mean, don't you think?'

'**Quite true.**' The pony nodded. '**Sorry. Not very nice of me, Clod-foot. But I mean, really! Look what you've done! Totally ruined my lemon meringue. Or at least the middle bit is done for. Still, I might be able to salvage some of the tasty bits from the edges . . .**' The pony began to lick the lemon cream off the straw. '**Mmmmmmm! Lemony goodness!**'

He was so busy hoovering up the spilt squishy filling that it took him a moment to notice that Eliza was staring at him with her mouth wide open in shock.

'**Hello? Yes?**' the pony said. '**Is something wrong?**'

'Ummm, I'm sorry, but who are you?'

The pony gave a hoot and kicked up his hooves as if this was the most hilarious joke. **'Who am I? Why, just a moment ago you were telling old Clod-foot here that I was your favourite pony in the whole of Pemberley Stables!'**

'Prince?' Eliza gasped. If she wasn't already a ghost, she would have turned pale with shock. 'But it can't be you!'

'It is I, indeed!' Prince took a deep bow in front of the girls. **'Sweet Prince, fastest steeplechaser in Pemberley. And what is your name? You - Clod-foot here! Speak up and introduce yourself!'**

'Um, I'm Olivia.'

'I think I prefer "Clod-foot".'

'Actually, I'd rather you called me Livvy,' Olivia said. 'That's what my friends call me . . .'

Eliza was still gaping in shock. 'But you can't be

my Prince! You look so . . . different!'

Prince shook his mane and laughed again as he swished his tail, thumping it on either side of his enormous belly. **'Well, yes, I suppose I have put on a few pounds since I saw you last! It's the witch's curse, you see – I can't help myself. One day I was as sleek as an otter and the next, *hey presto!* I had taken a liking to food, all sorts of sweet, sugary things, and before I knew it I had puffed up like so much flaky pastry on a sausage roll!'**

'The curse must have made you greedy,' Olivia realised, muttering under her breath.

'What was that?' said Prince.

The two girls looked at each other.

'Greedy . . .'

'Hmmm,' Prince mused. **'"Greedy" is a little harsh, don't you think? I mean, who doesn't love a scrummy cake?'**

♥ 26 ♥

Eliza's eyes narrowed. 'Where on earth did you get a lemon meringue pie from anyway?'

As if in answer to that question, yapping and scuffling started in the corridor outside Prince's stall. The girls stuck their heads out to see the rather rotund figure of none other than Horace the Hunt Master and his madcap pack of ghost hounds. As usual Horace was dressed in his red hunting jacket and his head was jiggling

all over the places. In that fateful hunting accident two hundred years ago, Horace had broken his neck in the fall when Eliza's pony had cut him off just before the hedge, and now, out of spite, the Hunt Master haunted Spellbound Stables. He was determined to keep the poor ponies cursed and had come up with all sorts of wicked tricks to do so.

Horace strode through the cobbled corridor, whistling a tune. In his arms, he carried a very large box.

'Prince, my good fellow!' Horace boomed. 'I come with treats!'

'Oh, what-ho, Horace!' Prince swished his tail with glee. **'Thank heavens you've arrived. You know, I haven't eaten a thing since breakfast.'**

'It's only nine o'clock!' Olivia pointed out.

'Is it really?' Prince swung round merrily. **'That's well past my morning teatime! Come on, my**

fox-master general, let's see what's in the box!'

Horace laid it on the floor in front of the hungry

pony and opened the lid to reveal . . .

'Croissants!' Prince's eyes lit up. **'Oh, *oui, oui*!!**

Croissants are my favourite!'

'With lots of different fillings,' Horace said. 'Three

chocolate ones, two

almond, four sugar-

topped, and six plain

ones fresh from the oven.

Which one would you

like?'

'Oh, all of them,

I should think!'

Prince said

cheerfully.

'All of them?' Olivia boggled. 'You can't eat

that many!'

'Ha! That's a bit rich coming from you, Clod-foot!' Prince scoffed. **'A girl who just stood in my pie and ruined my second breakfast!'**

Olivia was beginning to lose her temper with Prince. 'Lemon meringue pie is no breakfast for a horse. Hay is breakfast, or a nice bowl of pony nuts and oats. It's the witch's curse that makes you crave sweets!'

'Mhhits-umpblle!' Prince replied. Which Olivia took to mean 'It's possible', but it was hard to be entirely sure since the pony had just shoved two sugar-coated croissants into his mouth at once.

'So how do we break the spell?' Eliza wondered out loud.

'Get him to lay off the cakes?' Olivia suggested. 'After all, you said he was once a sleek athlete. Surely the key to breaking the curse is to get Prince on the straight and narrow and back in shape to race again?'

'Ha ha ha! Fat chance of that!' Olivia and Eliza turned round to see Horace chortling. 'The Grand National is in just two weeks,' the Hunt Master crowed. 'And, now that the witch's spell has made Prince too fat to run, my own horse, the Mischief Maker, is the hot favourite . . .'

'Oooh, did you say "hot favourite"?'

Prince put down his croissant and Olivia thought that perhaps there was a glimmer of hope that the pony might come to his senses at the thought of being beaten in the Grand National. **'I'd love a whole box of hot favourites right now!'**

'This is a nightmare! Eliza groaned. 'My handsome Prince has become a greedy glutton.'

'And if he doesn't change his ways,' Olivia agreed, 'that's one more pony that will stay trapped in time. Spellbound Stables could stay cursed forever.'

Chapter Three

Olivia came home from the stables to find her sister,
Ella, in the kitchen having a meltdown.

'Oh no! A soggy bottom!' she was wailing to their
mum.

'It's not that bad.' Mrs Campbell was trying to
soothe her oldest child. 'I think you can still eat it!'

On the table in front of them sat a tart covered
with gooseberries.

'It's not good enough for the Cake-off, though,' Ella said. 'I'll have to make something else.'

'There's a cake-off?' Olivia said. 'On the telly?'

'In the village,' Mrs Campbell said. 'The Great Pemberley Cake-off.'

'First prize is a hundred pounds!' said Ella.

Olivia could scarcely believe what she was hearing! All the way home she had been worrying about how she was possibly going to pay for all the hay that Bess needed. Not only that, but if they did manage to unbind Prince from his spell, well, then there'd be another horse to feed. The Cake-off could be the answer!

'If there's a hundred pounds up for grabs, then I'm entering too!' Olivia announced.

'You?' Ella looked shocked. 'Ha! Don't be silly. You don't know how to bake!'

'How hard can it be to follow a recipe?' Olivia replied.

'Mum!' Ella looked furious. She always liked to be the best at everything. ' Tell Olivia she can't!'

'Of course your sister can enter,' Mrs Campbell said. 'I think it's an excellent idea, Livvy. Why don't you take a look through the recipe books and then we'll pop up to the shops and buy some ingredients?'

Olivia began to leaf through the cookbooks on her mother's shelf. 'Something nice and simple to begin with . . .' she mused. And then she found a chapter entitled 'Nice and Simple'.

'Scones!' she cried. 'With jam and cream.'

Ella rolled her eyes. 'Scones? You'll never win the Cake-off with a scone!'

'Don't discourage her,' Mrs Campbell said. 'Scones are a good start. The competition is still two weeks away.'

'That's not enough time for you to become a

super-baker like me!' Ella growled at Olivia as she wrote down the ingredients. 'You'll never win!'

In the village that day it was pandemonium! The rush of people reminded Olivia of when they'd lived in London.

'I've never seen the shops so busy!' Mrs Campbell said. 'The flour is almost gone. We got the last bag!'

It looked like the entire village was going to enter the Cake-off. People were already bustling about on the village green, preparing bunting and various decorations, underneath a big banner of a smiling picture of the judge, a bright-eyed, raven-haired woman named Cherry Berry.

'Oh, this will be exciting!' Mrs Campbell said as they walked by the banner. 'Cherry Berry is famous for being very tough. It'll take a master baker to impress her!'

At home, Olivia unpacked the groceries and got to work in the kitchen.

'I'll help if you want,' Ella said.

Olivia wasn't sure about letting her bossy big sister get involved, but she had never baked before.

'I'll read out the ingredients,' Ella said. 'You can put them all in the mixing bowl.'

Olivia turned on the oven to preheat, as the recipe suggested, and then scurried back and forth, measuring out ingredients and putting them into the bowl in the order that Ella told her.

'Flour first,' Ella said, 'then buttermilk.'

'Okay,' Olivia said, 'what next?'

'Ten tablespoons of salt,' said Ella.

Olivia frowned. 'That sounds like rather a lot.'

'That's what it says here,' Ella replied.

Olivia shrugged. 'Okay then,' she said, pouring the salt in.

When the scones were in the oven, she watched them bake through the oven door. The recipe had said they would rise up to be light and fluffy like clouds. But they looked like flat rocks.

'Well, it is a first effort!' Mrs Campbell said kindly as she fetched the jam and cream out of the fridge. 'Ella, would you like one?'

'Ummm, not for me,' Ella said, scampering out of the kitchen. 'Uhhh . . . I've had too much tart.'

Mrs Campbell put jam and cream on her scone and took a bite.

'Crikey! How much salt is in this?'

'Ten tablespoons,' Olivia replied. 'Just like Ella said it was in the recipe.'

'Ella! You've sabotaged your sister's baking!' Mrs Campbell called out. But Ella, knowing which side her scone was buttered on, had already gone.

Chapter Four

When Olivia arrived at Spellbound Stables the next morning, Prince's stall was empty and she could sense there was magic afoot. Sure enough, when she stepped inside the stall, a ghostly mist rose up, up, up past her ankles until she was covered from head to toe. And then, when it disappeared, Olivia found herself at a racetrack. There were horses on the track and jockeys on their backs dressed in old-fashioned jodhpurs and racing silks.

'Livvy!' Eliza was waving to her from the grandstand.

'Did you remember to bring a stopwatch and binoculars?' Eliza asked when Olivia reached her.

'Yes,' Olivia said, 'but where's Prince?'

'Here he comes!' Eliza pointed to the podgy pony waddling towards them across the fields. 'Oooh, it looks as though he's gained even more weight if that's possible. He looks a bit like a hot-air balloon on legs.'

'Prince! Where's your saddle?' Olivia asked him. 'We told you to come dressed in your race kit ready to train for the steeplechase.'

'Ah yes,' Prince said. **'Bit of a funny story there actually, Livvy. You see, I went to put it on this morning and, well, it was the darndest thing! Someone must have shrunk my girth because I couldn't get it done up!'**

'Someone sneaked in and shrank your girth?' Eliza repeated.

'I know!' Prince said. **'Imagine that!'**

'Or,' suggested Olivia, 'could it be, Prince, that you've got so greedy that it doesn't fit you any more?'

'Oh, I hardly think that's likely!' Prince scoffed. **'I looked in the mirror this morning and I thought to myself, now there's a fellow who's in fine fettle!'**

'Was it a fairground mirror?' Olivia asked.

'Now, now, Livvy,' Prince said. **'I know you think**

old Prince is out of shape, but when you see me strut my stuff on the racecourse today, you'll be surprised. I'm every bit as swift as I used to be. The Grand National is in the bag.'

'The only thing that appears to be in the bag,' said Olivia, 'is cream buns.'

She pointed to the knapsack that Prince was carrying. A baker's dozen of buns were indeed inside it and some of them were now spilling out on to the racetrack.

'Ah yes,' Prince said, picking one up and giving it an eager lick. **'Early start and all that, so I thought I ought to bring a pre-breakfast snack.'**

'Prince!' Olivia groaned. 'No more pre-breakfast snacks! No more post-breakfast snacks. No morning teas and no afternoon teas. No midnight feasts and no elevenses. You must stop indulging and start training!'

'All right, all right, steady on!' Prince said. 'If I can race round the track in record time, will you get off my back?'

'I can't get on your back,' Olivia pointed out. 'Your saddle doesn't fit, remember?'

'Good point,' Prince mused. 'Might be best if you sit this one out, Livvy. I'll do the race on my own and you can time me on the old stopwatch.'

'Let's get you lined up at the start then,' Eliza said. 'Once round the track is four furlongs. In the days before you were spellbound, you could do it in forty-five seconds.'

'That's very quick!' Olivia was impressed. 'Perhaps since you're out of shape, though, Prince, you could just try to gallop it in under a minute?'

'Nonsense, Livvy!' Prince hooted. 'I'm in tip-top form! You just watch. Why, I might even break my old record!'

'You might break something,' Olivia muttered, 'and that's what worries me.'

Prince lined up and Olivia readied her thumb on the stopwatch. 'On your marks, get set . . . go!'

'What-ho!' Prince cried. **'I'm off!'**

And with a leap he flung himself forward at a gallop. The girls watched him run, but he had only gone a couple of strides before he promptly stopped and began to waddle along again.

'What's he doing?' Olivia asked.

'Owww.' Prince was wincing. **'I've got a stitch!'**

'But you haven't even gone ten metres yet!' Olivia called out to him.

'I'm all right!' Prince yelled back. **'Recovery mode!**

Just give me a moment to catch my breath! There we go! I've got my second wind now! And we're off!'

The girls watched the hands on the stopwatch whirring around.

'How far has he got now?' Eliza asked, peering into the mist as Prince lumbered further along the track.

'He's at the hundred-metre mark,' Olivia said.

'And how long has it taken him so far?'

'Five minutes.'

'Hmmm,' Eliza said, 'that's a little slow, isn't it?'

Olivia gawped at her friend in disbelief. 'Yes, Eliza. In fact, the other horses would not only have finished the Grand National by now, they'd already be home with their feet up, watching the reruns on the telly.'

'Quite slow then,' Eliza mused. She peered out at the track again and her face fell. 'Oh. That can't be good.'

'What is it?' Olivia asked.

'He appears to be lying down now.'

Olivia sighed. 'Come on then. We'd better go and get him up again.'

By the time the girls reached Prince he was up on his feet, but he was very puffed and sweaty and he'd given up entirely on the gallops. Instead he seemed to be having a picnic with the remaining cream buns from his knapsack.

'Prince!' Olivia was furious. 'Put those buns down. You're supposed to be training.'

Prince gave a loud burp. **'Splendid idea, Livvy. Only, the thing is, I've just eaten rather a lot now and I really should let it digest. You shouldn't run on a full stomach because you might drown.'**

'You mean swim on a full stomach?' Olivia said.

'Swim, run, same thing!'

'I think it's true.' Eliza nodded. 'I've heard that somewhere too.'

'This is impossible!' Olivia groaned. 'Prince is utterly out of shape!'

'Despair not, Clod-foot!' Prince chortled. **'I'm the fastest horse in the county, remember? This is just a cream-filled setback. I'll be on top form tomorrow - you'll see.'**

Olivia sighed. 'Okay,' she agreed. 'I'll meet you here again tomorrow morning. But this time we train for real against other horses. No more buns. No more lie-downs. This is serious.'

'**Marvellous! Good show!**' Prince said. '**I won't fail again, Livvy. Word of honour.**'

Olivia was just about to leave when he called after her.

'**Oh, and, Livvy?**'

'Yes?'

'**Bring some morning tea for me tomorrow, will you?**'

Chapter Five

The next day at the stables, true to his word, Prince was ready and waiting to run when Olivia entered his stall. He wore a jaunty rainbow sweatband round his head and coloured bandages on his legs.

'Still no saddle?' Olivia asked.

'He can't quite squeeze into his girth,' Eliza confirmed.

'Then I'll run alongside him,' Olivia said.

'Is that so?' Prince was doing warm-up stretches. **'How jolly sporting of you, Livvy! Let's hit the track, Jack! I hope you can keep up with me!'**

'I'm sure I'll manage,' Olivia replied drily.

There were other horses and jockeys already on the track when they arrived. Olivia jogged out to join them with Prince at her side.

'Now,' Prince said to her, **'watch and learn, Livvy. I'll give these chaps a flash of my heels as I dash past them to the winning post.'**

But, when the barriers sprang open and the racing began, Prince didn't speed by the other horses at all.

'Why, it's as if I'm stuck in treacle!' he grunted as he lumbered on, while one by one the thoroughbreds swept past him.

'Dash it all! Stop doing that!' Prince panted as yet another pony flitted by and left him behind in its wake.

'Is there something wrong?' Olivia asked.

'I should say so, Clod-foot!' Prince puffed. 'It's not very nice to be left in the dust when you were once the fastest horse on the track.'

Olivia smiled. Their plan was working.

'Would you like to be the fastest again, Prince?' she asked him. 'Because if you let us train you, I'm sure we can get you fit.'

'And then I'll be speedy again?' Prince asked.

'Then you'll be speedy again,' Olivia confirmed.

'What-ho! An excellent plan!' Prince agreed. **'I am your humble servant, Livvy.'**

'Yay!' Olivia said. 'Of course you'll also have to give up all those sugary treats.'

'Oh yes, yes,' Prince replied. **'Absolutely! It's a done deal!'**

'So shall we train again in the morning?' Olivia asked.

'What? Tomorrow?' Prince looked shocked. **'I was**

hoping for a lie-in. I like to have a jam roll in bed on a Sunday with a hot chocolate and the papers.'

'No, Prince! No time for jam rolls!' Olivia told him. 'We have less than two weeks before the Grand National.'

'**Oh, very well!**' Prince said. '**I tell you what, Livvy, I'll let my girth out a notch and wear my saddle tomorrow and you can even ride me round the track if you like.**'

'That's an excellent idea!' Eliza agreed, suddenly popping up out of nowhere in a puff of mist.

'Yikes!' Olivia cried. 'I wish you wouldn't do that!'

'Sorry,' Eliza said. 'Didn't mean to startle you!'

'It's okay,' Olivia said. 'So now we all know the plan and it's agreed. Tomorrow we meet at dawn.'

The next day Olivia arrived to find Spellbound Stables spookily silent.

Eliza was puzzled. 'Come to think of it, I haven't heard boo out of Prince all morning.'

'And why is the door to his stall shut?' Olivia wondered aloud.

'Prince?' Eliza called.

'I think we'd better go in,' Olivia said. 'Are you ready? One, two, three!'

When the girls burst in through the door, the whole stall looked like a winter wonderland! The straw on the floor was completely covered in shimmering white dust, like a layer of freshly fallen snow. And lying in the middle of the floor, coated in the white powder too, with his enormous belly bulging out in all directions and his tiny legs poking straight up in the air, was Prince.

'It must be some kind of fairy dust. He's been enchanted!' Eliza gasped.

Olivia wasn't so sure. 'He's not enchanted,' she said. 'He's asleep.'

'Are you certain?'

'Look at him!' Olivia insisted. 'He's snoring.'

It was true. Prince was wheezing like an old set of bagpipes. With each wheeze his belly rose and fell, and then, snuffling like a truffle pig, the overstuffed pony gave an almighty burp.

'Hey, wait a minute! This isn't enchanted dust . . .' Olivia picked up a handful of straw and sniffed it. Then she stuck out her tongue and gave the sparkling snow a vigorous lick.

'Ewwww!' Eliza was utterly horrified. 'Livvy! What are you doing?'

'I knew it!' Olivia said brightly. 'It's powdered sugar.'

She saw clearly now what had really happened here, and it all pointed to Horace the Hunt Master.

'Icing sugar everywhere!' Olivia said. 'And look, Eliza, a stack of doughnut boxes right by the front door. He's gone and done it again! Taking advantage of a weak-willed, greedy pony! The minute our backs were turned, Horace was in here, bribing poor Prince with his yummy, sugary treats!'

'He's in a sugar daze! We need to wake him up!' Eliza said.

But Prince, glazed all over with sugar and stuck in his glucose coma, was almost impossible for the girls to rouse. In the end, Olivia had to resort to waving a custard-filled doughnut under his muzzle so that the scent of sweet pastry could penetrate his senses and bring him round.

'Look!' Eliza said. 'He's waking up at last.'

'Ooooh,' Prince was groaning. **'Too much jammy**

filling! Too much doughy goodness! Ooooh, my head! Ooooh, my aching tummy!'

'Prince!' Olivia exclaimed. 'How can you keep falling for this? You're supposed to be in boot camp! How will you be in shape in time if you keep falling for Horace's tricks and scoffing all sorts of junk food?'

'Oof!' Prince rolled over inelegantly on to his side. **'I know, I know, Livvy. But it was all so delicious. You know doughnuts are my absolute favourite . . .'**

As he spoke Prince valiantly attempted to stand up, but his tummy was so big now he couldn't even get his legs to touch the floor.

'Help me!' he shrieked. **'I'm beached like a whale!'**

'Good grief!' Olivia watched him in horror.

'This is a nightmare!' Eliza shook her head in despair.

'Ugh . . . might I have a little assistance here?'

Prince grunted as he managed to get his front hooves to the ground.

'I'll get behind you!' Olivia offered.

A lot of fuss followed, with Eliza offering advice, Prince scrambling and panting, and Olivia shoving and pushing him up by the rump, but eventually the girls managed to help him get all four legs on the ground. Prince was on his feet once more, but his belly sagged so low now that it very nearly touched the ground.

'We're done for,' Olivia said. 'He'll never get into shape in time for the Grand National now.'

'I admit it's a setback,' Prince agreed as he waddled about the loosebox. **'But you can rely on me, Livvy. I won't be fooled again!'**

'No, Prince,' Olivia said. 'This time it was my fault. Horace is trying to ruin our chances and we need to be on our guard. From now on I'm going to meet you here every morning and escort you to the track.'

And so the training regime began in earnest.
Each day Olivia would arrive at Prince's stall to
find a box of pastries that the Hunt Master had
sneakily deposited at Prince's doorway to tempt
him. She whisked these to the local soup kitchen
before Prince could even see them. Thus, with
Horace foiled, their workouts went ahead without
distractions. Prince's girth was getting tighter. One
hole, then two, three and four. And the time on
Olivia's stopwatch grew quicker with
every passing day.

'Will he be ready for the race,
do you think?' Eliza asked as
they watched Prince doing his
best to perform a mad gallop
round the track.

'He's getting faster,' Olivia said, 'but we haven't much time. The Grand National is next Saturday!'

And so was the Great Pemberley Cake-off. When Olivia wasn't hiding pastries from Prince, she was flinging buns in the oven and her baking was improving. But time was running out for her to prepare for the Cake-off and for Prince to be ready for the Grand National, and the stakes had never been higher. It was time to bring her A game. It was time to bake a cake.

Chapter Six

The recipe for the triple-apple upside-down pie-cake might as well have been written in Russian for all the sense it made to Olivia! There was so much still that she didn't know about baking. Yet it was the degree of difficulty that made it such a winner. After all, Cherry Berry was a master baker. She wouldn't be impressed by run-of-the-mill sponge cakes and flans. No. If Olivia was to win the hundred pounds, she was going to have to produce something spectacular. And the triple-apple upside-down pie-cake was spectacular indeed.

She had spent the entire day preparing. She had peeled the apples, buttered and sugared the cake tin. She had crimped the pastry base and whisked the batter. She watched through the glass of the oven door as the cake baked with a golden-brown crust just as the recipe said that it should.

When she took the pie-cake out of the oven, the smell of sugary apples cooked into the bottom of the scrummy dessert was overwhelmingly delicious! Now all that remained was to make the cream-cheese icing that would go on the top and Olivia's entry for the Cake-off would be ready.

Humming a merry tune to herself, Olivia put the cake on a wire rack just as the recipe suggested and left it on the windowsill to cool while she went off to prepare the icing.

She was mixing the cream cheese with maple syrup and lemon when Eliza appeared beside her in the kitchen.

'Crikey!' Olivia shrieked and nearly dropped the mixing bowl.

'Sorry!' Eliza smiled. 'I keep doing that, don't I?'

'Yes, well, please don't!' Olivia said. 'Things have just reached a crucial point and I can't afford to make any mistakes.'

As soon as the words came tumbling out, she regretted snapping at her best friend. 'I'm sorry, Eliza,' Olivia said. 'It's just that I want so desperately to win this. Imagine! A hundred pounds would keep Bess in hay for absolutely ages . . . and any other ponies we might rescue.'

'If we manage to free them and bring them back to life,' Eliza pointed out.

'We will,' said Olivia.

She was brimming with positivity today and not just because of the pie-cake. After being fooled by Horace for so long, Prince had pulled his socks up. He had put in an excellent day's training yesterday. He'd been so fast on the track that he had broken his all-time record. The pony was well and truly back in shape and ready for the race. As for Horace, his attempts to lure the pony into overindulging seemed to have stopped.

'I haven't seen any sign of him in days,' Eliza said. 'I think he's given up trying to tempt Prince.'

In fact, Horace had not given up at all. As the girls laughed and chatted and stirred the cream-cheese icing, Horace was at that very moment outside Olivia's kitchen window, taking the cake.

'Prince! I come bearing the sweetest of treats!'
Horace boomed as he entered the stables.

'I say!' Prince stuck his nose out of his stall and
sniffed the air. **'Do my nostrils deceive me? Is that a
scrum-diddly-umptious triple-apple upside-down
pie-cake?'**

'Indeed it is!' Horace confirmed. 'Plucked fresh from a windowsill!'

'From a windowsill?' Prince mused. **'You don't suppose it belongs to someone?'**

'Oh, I doubt it!' Horace blustered. 'Why leave it there if not for me to snatch?'

'True. True!' Prince agreed. **'Good point well made, Horace! Oh, well then, as you say, apple-bottoms up!'**

Back in Olivia's kitchen, the girls were hunting high and low for the missing cake.

'Cakes don't just disappear,' Olivia said.

'They do if you eat them,' Eliza pointed out.

And then, in unison, they both cried, 'Prince!'

Olivia and Eliza came dashing into the stall, but it was too late! Prince already had his face planted in crumbly, appley goodness.

'Oh, it's the girls!' Prince cried. **'I say, you really must try this triple-apple upside-down pie-cake! It's quite the best thing I've ever tasted.'**

'My cake!' Olivia wailed. 'Prince, how could you? I was going to enter that in the Cake-off!'

'Your cake?' Prince was horrified. **'Horace told me it was up for grabs!'**

'And you believed him?' Eliza shook her head in dismay. 'Prince, really! When are you going to learn?'

'Well, right this minute, I should think!' Prince said. **'Fool me once, shame on you. Fool me an endless number of times – well, you get the picture. It's not going to happen again, girls. You have my word. I'm going to stop eating all the pies. I'll be ready to race.'**

'And what about the cake?' Eliza said.

'**Oh, I dare say I can fix it!**' Prince said. '**Look! If we just squish it all together again and you plaster the icing over the top, it will be just like new.**'

Olivia peered at the cake. 'It's got tooth marks in it.'

'**Hmmmm,**' Prince said. '**Has it? Might be tricky to disguise those.**'

Olivia prodded the cake on the plate. 'It's hopeless,' she said. 'I can't patch it up again. It's covered in pony slobber for starters.'

'Oooooh! Brilliant!' Eliza squealed.

The other two turned to her with incredulous expressions.

'Not the bit about the slobber,' Eliza said. 'I meant to say I've had an idea. A brilliant idea!'

Olivia and Prince looked even harder at her.

★ 69 ★

'I know, I know,' Eliza agreed. 'It's not usually me who comes up with a plan, but just this once I do happen to have one. And I'm pretty certain it's very good.'

'Well, go on then,' Prince said. **'Don't keep us in suspense, Eliza. Do tell!'**

'I happen to know where to find a recipe for a very special dessert that is bound to win the competition,' Eliza said.

'That would be brilliant!' Olivia agreed.

'But it's going to be tricky . . .' Eliza admitted.

'A bit of a snag, eh?' Prince said.

'Yes,' Eliza agreed. 'A bit.'

'Eliza,' Olivia said, 'where exactly is this recipe?'

'Well, that's the catch, you see,' Eliza replied. 'It's a two-hundred-year-old family recipe. And it's in the family cookbook . . . which is kept in the family kitchen . . .'

Olivia gasped. 'You mean your old kitchen?'

'That's right,' Eliza said. 'Olivia, we need to sneak into Pemberley Manor.'

Chapter Seven

Pemberley Manor had once been Eliza's childhood home.

'But after the witch cursed the ponies I refused to go back,' Eliza recalled, 'so I live in the stables now, and Mama rattles about the mansion all on her own – well, except for her ghost hounds of course.'

'So it's a haunted house?' Olivia asked.

'I suppose so,' Eliza replied. 'Do you think that

would explain why nobody has ever moved in after us? Well, actually people do move in, but they only ever last a night. They leave again smartly, looking quite white with fright.'

Olivia wasn't at all surprised. The manor house was very spooky-looking, perched on the hill right behind the stables. It had clearly once been very grand, but for the past two hundred years it had been gathering dust and cobwebs.

'Mama never was very keen on housekeeping,' Eliza admitted as they stood on the doorstep. 'But she's an excellent baker. We need to go inside and find her recipe book. Come on!'

Olivia followed her friend up the steps to the front door.

'How do we get inside?' she asked. But, even as she said the words, Eliza had grasped the door handle and it had magically swung open. As they entered, the dust and cobwebs disappeared and the house was suddenly transformed! The colour magically returned to the old faded carpets and curtains, and there were vases of fresh lilies in every room.

'Come on!' Eliza said as she ran along the marbled hallway towards the west wing.

'This house is enormous!' Olivia panted as they ran past room after room.

'I suppose it is quite grand now that I think about it,' Eliza agreed. 'There are so many rooms that I never did find them all. Luckily I know where the kitchen is!'

Eliza and Olivia hurried past a grand dining room and an elegant ballroom until at last they reached the kitchen.

'This is amazing!' Olivia couldn't believe it. The kitchen was as big as her entire house. There were massive ovens and a pantry stocked with ghostly goods.

'Here are the cookbooks,' Eliza said. She ran her fingers along the spines lined up on the shelf. 'It's not here,' she said with a sigh.

'Is the recipe in another book maybe?' Olivia asked hopefully.

'No, it's Mama's very own creation,' Eliza explained. 'Her cookbook is the one that I want.'

'You keep looking for it in here,' Olivia said, 'and I'll hunt through the other rooms in the house.'

'Try the library first,' Eliza called after her. 'Two doors down the hall to the left!'

The library was panelled in dark walnut, with overstuffed velvet sofas in shades of crimson, saffron and gold. The floor was carpeted in a rich emerald green and the shelves were crammed with every kind of book imaginable. Olivia began to search through them. She looked at book after book, but the cookbook simply wasn't there! She was about to leave when, out of the corner of her eye, she spied a book teetering on the edge of the very tippy-toppest shelf, so high up that Olivia had to climb the library ladder to reach it.

When her fingers grasped it at last, it was covered in ancient, ghostly sparkling dust. She blew it off the cover and saw that the jacket had nothing written on it at all. The book was wrapped in plain brown paper, dog-eared and worn as if it had been much loved at one time.

Olivia opened it, wondering if it might be blank inside too, but it wasn't. There were words on the first page.

MIDNIGHT MACARONS

Two ounces of wild strawberries, halved
One pound of fairyfloss sugar
Three midnight jasmine flowers
One French vanilla twill

Olivia flicked on to the next page and then the next. This was it! She had found Lady Luella's cookbook!

Clasping the book to her chest, Olivia was about to leave the library and race back to the kitchen when she heard footsteps in the hallway. Not Eliza's footsteps, but the mad scramble of paws. And then she heard a strange ghostly whining and yelping and her blood ran cold. Lady Luella's hunting hounds!

Still holding on to the cookbook as if her life depended on it, Olivia vaulted over the crimson velvet sofa and crouched down behind it. She hid there, her heart pounding, as she heard the hounds bound past the library door. Then Olivia felt the strangest sensation. Something hot and wet was trying to lick her foot. She turned round and saw one of the ghost hounds sniffing and slobbering his ghostly hot breath all over her! It was quite the most unusual, icky sensation!

'Stop it!' she hissed. 'Go away!'

From the other side of the sofa she heard the unmistakable cut-glass voice of Lady Luella. 'Freddie? What are you doing behind the sofa? Come out, you naughty hound!'

Desperate to see what was going on, Olivia popped her head up just long enough to clap eyes on Lady Luella. Eliza's mother was a ghostly beauty, with alabaster skin, russet hair and scarlet lips. Her dark eyebrows arched imperiously as she peered about the room. Olivia ducked back down again. Had she been seen?

And then, to Olivia's horror, a ghostly hand appeared round the arm of the sofa.

For a moment Olivia felt the air turn to ice around her as Lady Luella's elegant fingers reached towards her. And then the fingers grasped Freddie's collar and the hound gave a yelp as he was scooped up.

'Behave, Freddie!' Lady Luella scolded. Then she and her naughty hound departed and Olivia was alone once more.

She stayed behind the sofa a moment more, panting and trembling, then stood up and bolted back to the kitchen with the cookbook in her hands.

Eliza was delighted. 'Oh hooray! You've found it!'

'And your mama almost found *me*!' Olivia hissed. 'Lady Luella is here with her hounds! Quick, Eliza! We have to go!'

'Wait! Wait!' Eliza said. 'Give me the book!'

'What?' Olivia couldn't believe her ears. 'No! We have to leave!'

'Just let me find the recipe!' Eliza insisted. 'I want to gather a few secret ingredients from the pantry.'

Olivia handed the book over and waited with her pulse pounding in her temples as Eliza flipped through the pages and then went to the pantry and gathered the items she needed.

'I have them!' she squeaked. 'Let's go!'

Olivia began to head for the front door, but at that moment they heard the hounds.

'No! This way!' Eliza whispered. 'We can go out through the maids' entrance at the back.'

And so the girls slipped out through the scullery and into the herb gardens and past the chicken coop.

'Oh! Let me just get some eggs!' Eliza said excitedly.

'There's no time!' Olivia cried. But Eliza was

already poking about in the chicken coop. There was much fluttering and flapping and disgruntled clucking, but, when she emerged, she was clutching six eggs in the crook of her elbow. Their shells were a very pretty pink.

'Aren't they glorious?' Eliza cooed. But there was no time for Olivia to answer. The hounds had caught their scent again and were baying and scratching at the back door to be let loose. It was only a matter of time before Lady Luella would follow them.

'Heavens!' Eliza said. 'Run!'

So they did.

Chapter Eight

Olivia could scarcely contain her excitement as they arrived back at the stables. They had the recipe book, plus all the ingredients they needed from Lady Luella's pantry! Nothing could stop them now!

Except . . .

'What's that noise?' Olivia asked.

Dah-duh-da-duh-duh-dah-dun-dun-dan-dah!

'It sounds like a bugle!'

Eliza suddenly turned even more ghostly pale than usual.

'It's the "Call to the Post"!' she cried. 'That's the music they play when the Grand National is about to start!'

'The race?' Olivia said, confused. 'It's starting?'

'Right now, I should say,' Eliza confirmed. 'Quick! Prince needs to saddled up and ready to race.'

But when they entered Prince's stall they were in for a shock.

'No need to panic, girls!' Prince said. **'I'm ready! All kitted out!'**

'Oh my!' Eliza said. 'Prince! You see, Livvy? I told you he was amazing!'

Prince did look amazing. He was back in prime racing condition, sleek and powerful. His dark brown coat looked as if it had been polished until it gleamed, his black mane and tail were super shiny and the racing cloth beneath his saddle blanket shimmered in the Pemberley Stables colours of green and gold.

'You certainly look ready to win,' Olivia agreed.

'I am indeed!' Prince enthused. **'There's just one small snag-a-roo.'**

'And what's that?' Olivia asked.

'I don't have a rider.'

'Oh. That's definitely a snag-a-roo,' Olivia agreed.

'No. It's not,' Eliza said. The other two turned to her.

'Well, I seem to be the only one who has any clever ideas at the moment.' Eliza rolled her eyes at them. 'Come on? Isn't it obvious? Olivia should ride!'

'Me?' Olivia squeaked. 'But I've never ridden in a race before!'

'Old Clod-foot has a point,' Prince agreed. **'The**

Grand National isn't for beginners, you know, Eliza. The jumps are terrifying!'

'Livvy can do it,' Eliza said. 'She's very brave. Aren't you, Livvy?'

Olivia looked at Prince waiting expectantly in his glamorous kit. He had worked so hard to give up his cakes and get in shape. If she didn't ride in the race, it would all be in vain and the stables would remain spellbound forever.

'I'll do it!' she agreed.

'Oh hooray!' Prince cried. **'Good for you, Livvy. Right-ho, climb aboard!'**

'What, now?'

'I should think so,' Prince said. **'The race awaits!'**

Olivia clambered up into the saddle and, as she did so, the mist began to rise around them until soon it filled the whole of Spellbound Stables.

And then, a moment later, the mist cleared and Olivia found herself still on Prince's back – except now they weren't in the stables but on a racetrack, surrounded by other horses and riders, and Olivia was dressed just like Prince, in racing silks of gold and green.

A race steward was calling to her. 'Into the barrier, number twelve! We're about to start!'

'Oooh, we've got the number one inside track!' Prince was delighted. **'That's the best position to begin a race! Come on, Livvy! In we go!'**

They trotted up to take their place, but at the very last minute another rider in bright red silks cut them off and took it instead. As he whipped in front of her, Olivia thought there was something strangely familiar about him. He seemed suspiciously rotund for a jockey. Those red silks made him look like an overcooked saveloy.

'I say!' Prince snorted. **'Foul play! You stole our**
spot!'

The rider in the red silks turned round. 'The rules
are for fools!' he cackled. 'I'm in it to win it!'

'Horace!' Olivia was horrified. It was the Hunt
Master himself, mounted on his nasty-looking
chestnut steed, the Mischief Maker.

'**Fear not, Livvy,**' Prince said as he took up the one vacant space left in the barrier right alongside Horace and the Mischief Maker. '**Horace doesn't stand a hope against yours truly!**'

'What's he up to?' On the sidelines, Eliza was watching through her binoculars as the Hunt Master slipped his hand inside his silks. 'He's taking something out . . . Oh no! It's a jam-filled cream bun!'

Horace whipped out the bun and stuck it on the barrier gate right in front of Prince's nose.

'**Oh, I say!**' Prince said. '**A bun! Very kind of you, fox-master general!**'

'No, Prince!' Olivia cried. 'Don't eat it! Can't you see he's trying to tempt you so that you get distracted and lose the race?'

'**Oh, ha ha ha! Livvy, please!**' Prince said as he reluctantly put aside the jammy cream bun with a dreamy look of longing. '**I wouldn't fall for a**

ridiculous ruse like that!'

'But, Prince,' Olivia shrieked, 'you already have! While you've been ogling the bun, the other horses have gone!'

It was true! The start gates had already sprung open and the horses were off!

'Never fear!' Prince said valiantly. **'We'll catch them! Hang on, Livvy!'**

And, with that, they were off and racing.

Olivia hastily put her goggles on to stop the mud from the other horses' hooves blinding her as they fell in behind their stride and galloped on.

'Jump ahead!' Prince yelled. **'Grab my mane, Livvy!'**

The horses bounded over the first jump like stags. Prince was lagging behind the others, but he was swifter than the rest of the pack by far and had more experience than any of them, so he was gaining fast.

Prince flew over the next hedge, and the one after that too.

'Prince is in the middle of the field,' the commentator cried, 'and he's gaining fast on the leader, the Mischief Maker.'

'Go on, Prince!' Eliza screamed from the sidelines.

Prince needed no encouragement. He was flying now!

'**Ahoy-hoy!**' he cried. '**We have them in our sights, Livvy! The race is ours!**'

But then suddenly, instead of mud flying up into Olivia's face, something else struck her goggles. Something white and wiggly.

'Crikey!' she said, wiping them clean. 'Whipped cream!'

Horace was up to his old tricks again, throwing buns. He landed one directly in front of Prince, but Prince ignored it and kept running.

The end of the race was in sight now . . . but the buns kept coming! Horace was throwing more and

more of them on to the track to tempt poor Prince!

Then, from out of nowhere, came the baying of hounds and suddenly Freddie, Lady Luella's naughty hunting dog, swept ahead of them and gobbled up the bun. He ate the next one that Horace threw too, and the one after that. All the tempting treats were soon out of the way!

Olivia found herself clutching Prince's mane for dear life as the spellbound pony leaped forward and began to pass the other horses. As the winning post loomed, only Horace was ahead of them.

'He's out of buns!' Eliza was yelling from the sidelines. 'There's nothing to stop you now! Run, Prince! Run!'

'Come on, Prince!' Olivia was shouting too. 'You can do it!'

With a leap and a bound they crossed the line and the commentator called out over the tannoy, 'Prince!

Prince has crossed the finishing line first!'

Prince had done it. They had won the Grand National!

Chapter Nine

In the winner's circle Prince pranced about in delight as a wreath of yellow roses was placed round his neck.

'Oh, they smell scrumptious and sweet!' Prince exclaimed, but Olivia noticed that for once the pony didn't try to eat them.

Olivia had only just leaped off Prince's back to weigh in on the jockey scales when it happened.

At first she thought it was the flashbulbs from the cameras going off all around that were making Prince glow, but the light was far too powerful for that. It was as if the sun itself were shining its rays down on the sleek and splendid pony. **'Oh, what-ho! Look at me glow!'** Prince cried. And then the light seemed to knock him clean off his feet because he began rolling about on the ground, tossing this way and that.

'Help me, Livvy! What's happening to me?' Prince wailed. **'I feel very peculiar! It reminds me of that time I ate two dozen jam tarts . . .'**

Eliza came running up to join Olivia and the two girls watched as the deep magic took hold.

'It's okay, Prince,' Olivia said. 'It's the spell. You've broken it! You're being transformed!'

'Well, I can't say I like it much!' Prince said. **'It feels all tingly and . . .'**

And at that moment he stopped talking and all

that came out of his mouth was a whinny!

'It's happened!' Olivia said. 'He's not enchanted any more. He's a real-life pony again!'

So one more of the ponies trapped by the Pemberley Witch's spell had been set free.

'Isn't it brilliant?' Eliza trilled as Olivia put Prince back into his stall beside Bess's. 'Hooray for us!'

Olivia, meanwhile, was transfixed by the real-life Prince.

'He's so beautiful,' she breathed in admiration. 'No wonder he was your favourite, Eliza.'

'Oh yes,' Eliza agreed. 'He's a terrific pony, very swift. You'll have such fun riding him, Livvy.'

Olivia stroked Prince's velvety muzzle. 'Do you hear that, Prince? We're going to have fun together, you and me.'

Prince stamped a hoof. And then he swished his tail. It was clear that being unable to speak was making him cross.

'What do you think he's trying to say?' Olivia asked.

'I should think he's hungry,' Eliza said. 'Even before he was enchanted, Prince had a handy appetite on him.'

'Shall we give him some hay then?' Olivia asked.

She gave Prince a biscuit of hay and the pony promptly ate it. She gave him another biscuit and he ate that too. And then a third and a fourth.

'Goodness,' Eliza marvelled as Prince worked his way through the better part of a bale of hay. 'You really need to win that baking competition now if we're going to keep him well fed.'

'The baking competition!' Olivia squeaked. 'I'd totally forgotten about it! It's today!'

'We have to hurry,' Eliza said. 'Quick! Let's go to your house with the ingredients and bake!'

Luckily for the girls, by the time they made it home to Olivia's, the house was empty. There was a note from Mrs Campbell on the fridge.

Gone to the village to
watch the judging!
See you there!

'We're too late!' Eliza wailed.

'No!' Olivia insisted. 'We still have an hour before the entries close.'

'There's barely enough time,' Eliza said. 'The pavlova takes almost that long to prepare.'

'What's a pavlova?' Olivia asked.

'Oh, it's the most amazing dessert that my mama

used to bake,' said Eliza. And she turned the pages to
the recipe in the book.

PINK PAVLOVA WITH SUGAR VIOLETS

'All the ingredients are here,' Eliza said as
Olivia unpacked the box that they had taken from
Lady Luella's pantry. 'Including the special secret
ingredient – pink eggs from my mama's prize-laying
hens.'

'This looks very complicated,' Olivia said, reading
through the recipe. 'I don't even know what half
these things are!'

'I've made it before,' Eliza assured her. 'I'll do the
directing and you do the baking.'

'*Two brave girls*,' Olivia agreed. 'Just like the spell
says.'

The girls worked in the kitchen at lightning speed.

Olivia didn't stop to think; she simply did whatever Eliza told her to, beating the pink egg whites until they formed rose-tinted peaks, then adding glittering spoonfuls of fairyfloss sugar and baking it in the oven before topping it all off with snowy mountains of whipped vanilla cream and delicate, shimmery, sugar-coated violets.

The finished dessert looked quite magical. *Maybe a little too magical*, Olivia thought. What would the pavlova taste like?

'Shall we try it, do you think?' Eliza asked.

Olivia looked at

the clock on the wall. 'There's no time!'

With the pavlova stuffed hastily in a cake box they raced out of the door. Would they make it to the Cake-off in time?

Chapter Ten

In a pop-up marquee in the middle of the village green, the final judging of the Great Pemberley Cake-off had begun.

The trestle tables were groaning under the weight of almost a hundred cakes, and for hours now Cherry Berry had been moving back and forth down the rows, prodding, poking and tasting.

Finally, she had narrowed them down to four. Her

favourites were a chocolate jam sponge roll, a marble layer cake, a peanut-butter-and-marshmallow slice and a red velvet cake. It was to the red velvet cake that she now turned her attention once more. She took a forkful, held it up to scrutinise it and then, with gusto, she gobbled it down.

'Who made this?' she asked.

Ella Campbell stepped forward. 'Me, Cherry!'

'Young lady, this cake is a triumph!' Cherry Berry announced. 'It has excellent texture. No soggy bottom! And how did you get it such a lovely deep red?'

'I used beetroot,' Ella replied triumphantly.

The crowd gasped. Beetroot? How controversial!

'Well done!' Cherry Berry replied. 'Beetroot is quite the right answer. A real red velvet cake uses the natural colour of beets instead of fake food colouring.'

Ella was looking as smug as a bug now. Cherry Berry was lavishing praise on her and reaching for the red rosette.

Ella was extra-smug because, while it was true that she'd used beetroot, she had also cheated with a packet of cake mix. But it looked like she'd got away with it. Cherry Berry had been tricked and she was going to scoop the big prize!

Cherry Berry was about to pin the first-place rosette on the cake when . . .

'Please! Wait!'

Olivia came running into the marquee with the cake box under her arm.

'Is there still time?' she panted. 'I have a pavlova I'd like to enter.'

'It's over, twerp!' Ella hissed at her. 'It's done and I've won!'

But Cherry Berry's interest had been piqued.

'Pavlova, you say?' She peered at the box in Olivia's hands. 'A very difficult feat to pull off! A complexity factor of level ten! I should very much like to see it. Bring it out then, young lady, and pop it on the table!'

The pavlova trembled as Olivia lifted it from the box. At first Olivia thought it was because she was shaking with nerves. But then she realised it was the pavlova doing it all by itself. The dessert seemed to wiggle and wobble in a spooky fashion. And it sparkled too, in a very otherworldly way, almost as if it was enchanted – which, Olivia supposed, it actually was. After all, she had used eggs from Lady Luella's haunted hens to bake it. And the violets and the fairyfloss sugar had come from the spooky pantry at Pemberley Manor.

'What an incredible shade of pink this pavlova is!' Cherry Berry cooed. 'I've never seen anything like it in all my life!'

She went to stick her fork into the pavlova and had to make a couple of attempts because somehow the pavlova kept dodging out of her way, but in the end she managed to scoop a good amount on to the tines. As the crowd watched, she raised the fork to her mouth and took a bite. Cherry Berry's eyes widened.

Olivia's heart was pounding. The crowd were

hushed in anticipation.

'Why, I've never before tasted anything like it!' Cherry Berry marvelled. 'It's so light it's as if it isn't even there! The sugary sparkles disappear on your tongue like sweet fog! It's utterly spine-tingling!'

Cherry Berry turned to Olivia. 'What is the name of your miraculous confection?' she asked.

'Pardon?' Olivia said.

'Your dessert –' Cherry Berry repeated the question – 'what do you call it?'

'Oh,' Olivia said, 'um . . . Ghost Pavlova!'

'Ghost Pavlova!' Cherry Berry exclaimed. 'That's exactly what it tastes like! What a winner!'

She took the red rosette and pinned it on the pavlova and handed Olivia a hundred pounds. 'You simply must give me your recipe!'

Olivia smiled. 'I can't, I'm afraid, Miss Berry. It's a family secret.'

Ella glared at her sister. 'We don't have a pavlova recipe!'

'I didn't say it was *our* family secret,' Olivia replied as she pocketed the money.

'Where are you going now?' Ella cried.

'I'm off to buy some hay,' Olivia replied. It was nearly suppertime and she had hungry horses to feed.

'Eliza?' Olivia called as she pushed open the stable doors. 'Eliza? It's me! We won!'

'Oh, hooray!' Eliza exclaimed as she appeared out of nowhere.

For once, Olivia wasn't the least bit startled. The two friends skipped and danced with joy and the horses joined in too, neighing over their stable doors as Olivia flung armfuls of hay into their racks.

'Now we have enough money to keep the ponies with full tummies,' Olivia said, 'there's absolutely nothing to stop us bringing the whole lot of them back to life!'

At these words, as if by magic a spooky mist rose up and the ghost hounds came bounding through the doors!

'Yikes!' Olivia scuttled to one side to get out of the way as Freddie came racing for her with his pink tongue lolling out. Behind the hounds, with the mist swirling round her long velvet skirts, was Lady Luella. She looked very ghostly indeed as she swept up to the girls and hovered in mid-air.

'Hallo, Mama,' Eliza said.

'Eliza!' Lady Luella raised an imperious eyebrow. 'I believe you have something that belongs to me?'

Eliza sighed and produced the cookbook, handing it to her mother.

'We were only borrowing it,' she insisted.

'It was to help the ponies!' Olivia added.

Lady Luella turned her ghostly gaze to Olivia.

'You, girl! You seem determined to meddle in matters that are none of your concern.' And then she added, 'You may have won the Grand National, but there are greater hurdles ahead. You do not yet understand the true nature of the witch's curse.'

As she said this last bit, Olivia saw Lady Luella exchange a mysterious glance with Eliza.

'One more spell you've broken,' Lady Luella said as she hovered. 'The other spells remain. You'll need all your wits about you to break the chain. Farewell,

Eliza, dear heart, until we meet again.'

And then, in a puff of spectral smoke, Lady Luella and the hounds were gone.

'What do you think your mother meant,' Olivia said, 'about the true nature of the curse?'

'Oh, nothing important I shouldn't think,' Eliza replied a little too hastily, and Olivia suspected that her friend might be keeping a secret too.

'Do you also think it was odd,' Olivia continued, 'how, in the race, Freddie swooped in to eat the buns? Is it possible that your mother's trying to help us? Do you think she wants us to succeed?'

'Well, Mama wasn't the one who actually cast the spell,' Eliza reminded her friend. 'It was the witch who did it, and you've heard her say the witch's spell is unbreakable. Even if Mama wanted to, she can't change it. The spell binds all of us, Mama included.'

'It's up to us then,' Olivia said. '*Two brave girls.*

We'll break the spell one pony at a time, and one day they'll all be free and you'll come to life, just like the ponies.'

Eliza said nothing, and Olivia could have sworn she saw tears glistening in her best friend's eyes. Then, with a shiver, Eliza pulled herself together and gave Olivia a smile. '*Two brave girls*,' she agreed. 'What do you say, Livvy? Are you ready for the next one?'

Olivia looked at sweet Prince, munching his hay happily in his stall. If he could still speak now, what would he have said?

'Oh, I should think so, Eliza.' She giggled. 'What-ho! Let's go!'

NEXT IN THE SERIES . . .

Wishes and Weddings

Olivia blinked in the darkness. 'Ooh, I'm blind as a bat! Where are the lights?' She flicked on the switch and gasped. 'Eliza? Where on earth is the pony? She's gone!'

The stall was completely empty . . . except for a giant heap of muck that had been dumped right in the middle of the room on top of the straw.

Eliza groaned. 'She's not gone at all. You're looking straight at her!'

And then Olivia saw that the mud heap was wobbling a little. Not just wobbling, but kind of jiggling and then . . . it spoke!

'Hello, babes!' the mud heap trilled.

'Eek!' Olivia shrieked. 'The mud just spoke to me!'

The mud heap began jiggling even harder at this and a cloud of dust rose up as it gave a tinkling laugh.

'Oh, babes! Me a mud 'eap? You must be joking! Whatever are you on about?' The mud heap moved closer to Olivia and out of the gloom of the stall and now she could see that it had legs! And eyes, and a muzzle!

'Livvy,' said Eliza with a sigh, 'this is Sparkle.'

'You mean underneath all that mud is a pony?' Olivia gasped.

'She never used to be like this,' Eliza said. 'I can remember her well.'

Olivia nodded. Of course Eliza would know what the pony had been like. They had once been her very own ponies – until the day she'd had a riding accident and died, and then her mother, Lady Luella, the owner of Pemberley Manor, had got the Pemberley Witch to put a curse on the ponies to punish them and they had been trapped in time.

'When Sparkle was a real-life pony she was brilliant white, well groomed and with a silken mane and lustrous tail that were the envy of all,' Eliza went on.

'Poor Sparkle!' Olivia said. 'The Pemberley Witch has turned her into a mud-caked mess!'

'Oooh, babes, don't worry.' Sparkle shook her dusty mane. 'You took Sparkle by surprise is all. Give me a quick minute to fix myself up a bit . . .'

The mud heap shambled off to the other side of the stall and dug about in the hay, and when she returned there was a tiara stuck sideways in her forelock and she had drawn all over her grubby muzzle with bright pink lipstick.

'There!' Sparkle said. 'Sparkle's all gorgey-porgey now! What do you reckon?'

'Uhhh, much better?' Olivia still couldn't quite believe her eyes.

'Come in, come in, and make yourself comfy!' Sparkle swished the muddy thicket that passed for her tail and gestured for Olivia and Eliza to join her.

'Sit down! Sit down!' Sparkle beckoned, and Olivia noticed now that the stall was more like a teenager's bedroom than a stable. There was a bed with a duvet with hearts and crowns all over it and the walls were smothered in pictures torn from magazines.

'This looks exactly like my sister Ella's bedroom!' Olivia said.

The posters on the wall all seemed to be of the same dark-haired boy. In the photos he was often doing very dashing things like sailing a ship or sword fighting or horse riding.

'Who's that boy?' she asked.

Sparkle chortled. 'Livvy, Livvy, Livvy! You've been living under a rock, babes! You must know Prince Patrick!'

'I'm afraid I don't . . .' Olivia replied. 'But you seem to like him a lot!'

'Oh, everyone loves Patrick,' Eliza agreed. 'He's very popular. Handsome, charming – you know, the usual stuff.'

'He's a dashing prince!' Sparkle confirmed. 'And now he's getting married!'

'So there's going to be a royal wedding,' Eliza said. 'And who is the bride?'

'Why the princess-to-be is Lady Petronella!' Sparkle cried. 'It's been in all the papers! They're completely over the moon in love! It's going to be the most amazey-mazey wedding dazey! I simply cannot wait! I am all lovey-la-la! Ding-dong! Wedding bells! Huzzah!' ...

To be continued ...

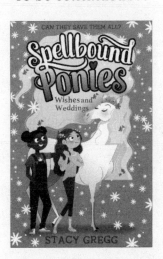

CAN THEY SAVE THEM ALL?

Spellbound Ponies

Wishes and Weddings

STACY GREGG

Out Now

CAN THEY SAVE THEM ALL?

Spellbound Ponies

Sugar and Spice

STACY GREGG

Out Now

CAN THEY SAVE THEM ALL?

Spellbound Ponies

Magic and Mischief

STACY GREGG

Collect

…them all!